DEATH & DEPRAVITY

ARUN THAKUR

Made with ♥ on the Notion Press Platform
www.notionpress.com

In the loving memory of my grandfather, a wise man

who led his life with dignity and faith.

Ad astra per aspera

Contents

Acknowledgements

I, first of all, will like to express my gratefulness to my grandparents for being the kind-hearted gentle humans they are and for always keeping me in touch with kindness. Secondly, I will like to express my gratitude to Fatima who being the innocent gracious person she is, supported me throughout writing this story, listened to my obscure philosophical ramblings, and even wrote the pages of Vijay's journal in her beautiful cursive handwriting. I would also like to thank my dear friend Kinshuk who sketched the wonderful intriguing picture "Visions of Death and Demons". Lastly, I will always be grateful for the lovely intelligent friends who discuss art, philosophy, poetry, and often random nonsense with me.

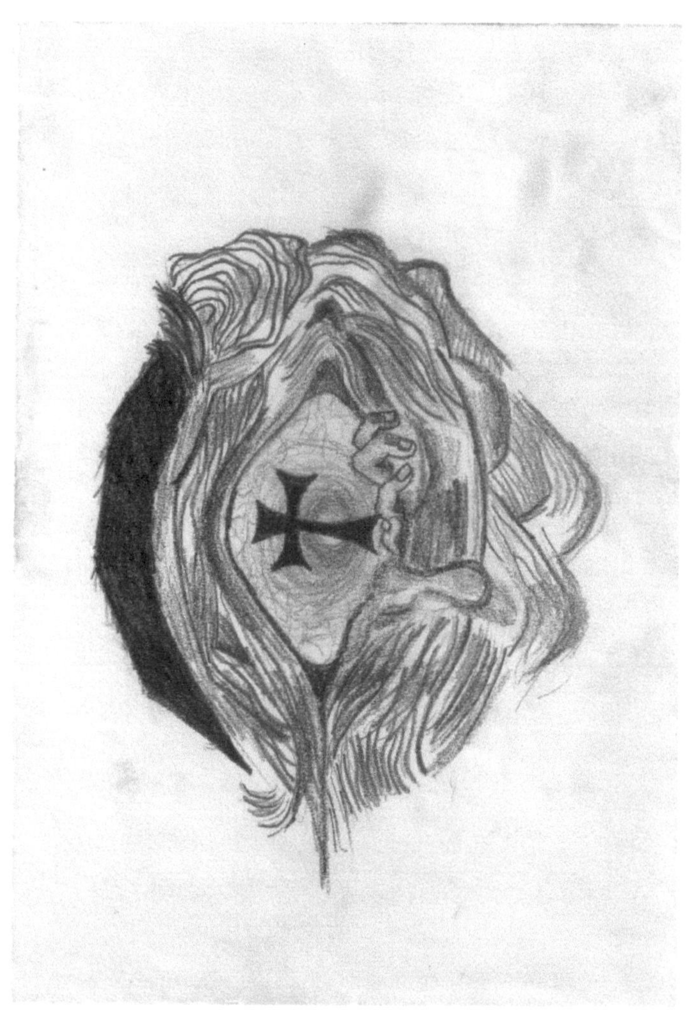

"Visions of death and demons" by **Kinshukleen kaur**

A Godless Man's Cry To God.

Oh, father art thou in heaven still?
or have thee left for a different dwelling
for look what suffering has fell upon us
thy children are evil and ill
Hollow is thy name for no good it's calling does
death and doom loom over us all
why thy miracles are only bestowed upon Lazarus?
Witness! How to sickness and suffering, we succumb
futile is thy tantalizing gift of life
for one goes through it in agony and pain
and even in death, finds no freedom
What a wretched pit has thy kingdom become!!
False is thy name and cursed is thy reign
but weak are we and thine is the glory
So it shall last forever and ever. Amen.

Prologue

July 14th 2015

Why have i turned to this forsaken journal after so many days of writing nothing?

No, I must not consent to it, it's not right I can't be so cruel and indifferent. There's still some hope. Yes, I must not give up so soon. Oh, but what good is this hope? Isn't hope just an illusion? Isn't the cause of all our miserable troubles is this expectation of a better future, a hope of some divine power to remove our suffering? How foolishly optimistic of us to think that in a box full of evil, a blessing lies at the bottom. Hope is no blessing, it's a curse! Yes, a curse, the vilest, most wretched, and most evil of them all. It does man no good. Mother has been hoping for months yet how miserably she weeps at night! Father hoped when he could think and what good this hope brought him. Nothing but slow suffering and pain. I hoped like a child for it to all be better, and now here I sit at late dark hours writing like a maniac. Yes, I must not leave it to hope anymore, I must not let it all happen just because our hearts are too afraid to look at the truth, for men who live on hope can never live in grace. I know nothing can change and I know there is no hope. I must not let this perverted game of hope and suffering go on any further. But isn't this all evil? Am I a shallow creature who can't even imagine the possibility of good? No, I mustn't delve into questions of morality now. I must bring this to its impending conclusion however undesired and devastating it may be. I must take action even if my actions are judged as evil, in the eyes of some indifferent egoistic god.

I

Walk

"You can't even trust life anymore, it's too feeble," said Kamala standing on the side of the narrow village path with a milk jug in one hand.

"Right! Poor Seeta Devi, I only met her yesterday and she looked fine to me, even on her last day she was walking with flowers in her hands, to the temple" replied Sushma who had stopped on her way to the field and found time out of her monotonous routine of grazing the cattle and watering her potatoes to gossip.

"She was old but never took a day's rest. I always saw her busy looking after her cows and reading her *Hanuman Chalisa*. What a good woman she was!" said Kamala with a tired face, wrinkled and dried by years of labor in the dust.

The conversation turned into incoherent noise as Vijay left the women behind and continued on his walk through the village. He had only reached his small village - 'HeerPur' situated on the top of a hill amidst, tall fir trees and a significant mass of land cleared out for farming after a day's train ride from the smoky, garbage-chocked corners of Delhi. The nearest town being fifteen kilometers away the village was considerably isolated and quiet with the people spending their days in the fields and forests.

He made this journey every year in February with his parents but this year had found himself alone in his travels, as his father had fallen ill with dengue and passed away in June, and he had just turned eighteen.

The purpose of these yearly visits was to stay with his grandparents for a few weeks and enjoy the quiet life of a small village. Of course, neither of those was possible anymore since his grandfather had passed away two years back due to old age, and the village was anything but quiet since the old Seeta Devi had passed away yesterday night. Now everybody was busy having conversations and gossiping about it. Even Vijay's grandmother had gone to Seeta Devi's small house to meet her son, his wife, and kids who lived in the city and had only come to Seeta's home after five years.

What good is their presence, now that the woman is dead? Crocodile tears don't bring back the dead, and where were the son's care and love for his unfortunate mother when she was alive?

Vijay thought to himself with the same frustration he had developed since his father's death. For months now his thoughts have been bitter and full of hatred, towards everything it seems, but he doesn't lets that affect his behavior with the simple people of his village. Who were always ready for small talk and quickly noticed the slightest hint of rudeness or dejection and went on to ask you more questions about it. So Vijay avoided appearing like the tired, frustrated guy he was since an interrogation about his mental state with some bored, nosy woman is the last thing he wanted.

Walking around the village was one of his favorite things to do although he rarely got out of his house. He had spent most of last year shut inside in his room in his city home, studying for his final high school exams and hating to walk out in the noise and traffic and talking with people. He especially hated the obnoxious way in which people talked to him as if he were a lost little boy who was too innocent to see the patronizing pity in their eyes whenever the topic of his father's death came up.

But today was different, he had decided to walk and observe anything and everything.

II

Ignorance

The sky was dull and grey with no sign of sun or any apparent dark rain clouds. It was just plain, empty, lacking any features that one could gaze upon as one wandered around aimlessly. The village was often grey and cold and it was colder still since winters were longer in the mountains and even lasted till march sometimes.

After walking for a few minutes Vijay reached in the central part of the village. The dirt path was the widest here and even cemented at some places since the sarpanch and most families of the village lived in this area.

He saw a woman in her forties coming in his direction, with a look in her eyes that signaled Vijay that she had already made up her mind to make small talk with him.

"Vijay, is that you? Oh look how you have grown" said the woman stopping next to him, with a smile on her face which seemed more like a learned habit, rather than a natural gesture.

In these moments Vijay always found himself at a lack of words. He never knew in what way he was related to the person standing next to him and how to address them.

And funnily enough, everybody was related to everybody, in some way or the other in the village. He never cared to remember all the aunts and uncles and cousins but always recognized their faces when he saw them. He always knew if he had seen the person standing next to him, in some event, and touched their feet as was the custom. Everybody was unknown to him, but not enough that they could be called strangers. Without giving any more thought to it, he slowly bent down and touched the woman's feet and avoided addressing her as anything specific "Yeah I have" he replied, with a practiced smile of his own.

"But oh my boy, how thin you have become! and even your face looks so bonny, the food in the cities is never good enough to keep anyone healthy and fit" said the woman with an animated expression and careless concern.

"I think it's for the good, I used to be too fat in childhood and nobody seemed to like that either" he replied with disinterest. He had been through this same conversation too many times, to even care about it anymore. He could never understand why people thought the best way to start a conversation, was by pointing out his skinny body and pale face.

"You are right too. Wait, if you are here who's with your mother in Delhi? Has she come too or is she all alone there?!" said the woman without mentioning his father. That's the one thing he liked about village folk, since his father's funeral had been held in the village with all the proper customs and a feast for the whole village after thirteen days, nobody talked about his death anymore. They had said their sorries and expressed their grief, and now the memories too suffered the same fate as the dead; left to rot and be forgotten.

"She had some work to tend to, so she's still in Delhi but her sister is there to be with her, so no she's not alone"

"oh okay, and what about your exams?"

"Sorry but" he interrupted "I was going to look for my grandmother, so I think I should be on my way now" he mustered up an excuse as he no longer wanted to spend more time being part of a conversation, where both parties pretended to be concerned about the tedious minor details of each other's lives and talking was done for the sake of talking. Words should always point towards something other than themselves, he believed.

"Yes, of course, I believe you'll find her at Seeta Devi's house, that's where other people have gathered too, to pay their respect." the woman said softly with a solemn face.

"Thank you," said Vijay and continued walking without looking back. Escaping conversations and avoiding social interactions was something he had become quite good at, over the past few months. People and their opinions and remarks frustrated him with their trivial nature. Sometimes even the simple act of standing and talking with someone made his heart anxious and irritated his mind.

He reached near a Cowpen. Nobody was around except the brown Sahiwal cow chewing on leaves, sitting inside the pen on soft green grass. Most people in the village had at least one cow, his grandmother too had one, and some even had three to four, if their families were larger with more young kids to drink the milk.

He always liked cows, not in the religious Hindu sense but just for their big innocent eyes and calm demeanor. Most people tended to only treat them for what they were, animals to be fed and milked. Nothing more, nothing less. Being emotionally attached to animals was not a prospect they cared much about. He lowered down and rested on his knee. Slowly, he moved his hand closer to the cow's head and started softly rubbing it with his fingers. The cow didn't seem to react much and carried on chewing on the dry fodder. Animals he thought were quite blissful, they were creations of nature as nature intended them to be. Human suffering was a virtue he liked to believe, but sometimes he thought that if a choice was given to him between being a conscious ape, born with the ability to think and toil and live his whole life grinding against the laws of nature, or being born an ignorant animal, feeding on what he wished and passing his days in harmony with the elements. He would choose ignorance in a breath.

"How happy is the blameless vestal's lot!
The world forgetting by, the world forgot
Eternal sunshine of the spotless mind!
Each pray'r accepted and each wish resign'd" -
Alexander pope

A mind turned into a white pure salt lake reflecting the eternal blissful light of a forgiving sun. The idea made him feel at peace sometimes. Of course, if he expressed these thoughts out loud, people would call it a pathetic notion, to forsake the wonderful blessing a human mind was and become a simple silent cattle. Oh, how stupid it was.

And maybe they were right, it was after all just a simple fantasy of a bored pessimistic mind, created to relieve itself of the exhausting toil that existence was. But, then again these simple stupid thoughts were a result of the divine consciousness he has been blessed with. It was quite paradoxical like all fantasies were. His fingers felt wet as the cow started licking them with its long bluish-black tongue and he snapped out of his confused thoughts.

III

Resentment

Wandering around in the cold with his hands hidden inside the deep pockets of his black warm jacket and neck wrapped with an old brown scarf; his grandfather's scarf, he had reached the dirt road which went straight down the hill and lead into a forest. Women often used this path, for collecting grass for the cattle from the forest and fetching fresh water from the small baori situated at about a ten minute walk down the hill. It was just a small tank with steps inside it, being filled with cold fresh water which seemed to magically appear out of the mountain rocks.

He stood in confusion about whether to walk down the hill or just sit there and gaze at the endless, green curious valley lying in front of his eyes.

His confusion was put to an end when someone tapped him on the back and greeted him with "where are you heading to ?" the voice belonged to Samiksh, a tall boy with rough brown hair and a wheatish lean face, wearing a faded old red sweater which his mother had probably knitted years ago for his older brother and now it had found its way onto his skinny but firm body. Samiksh was probably the only person in the whole village, whose company was tolerable to Vijay.

They only talked when Vijay returned to the village and never cared to keep in touch through social media. Conversing on texts was something Vijay had developed a disliking for and Samiksh never cared to indulge in.

"oh I was just walking around, but the bottles in your hands tell me you are heading down to the baori" replied Vijay with a smile.

"yes, come walk with me, it's a boring journey without company"

"Okay well" Vijay muttered softly and they naturally started slowly walking down the hill.

"So, the result will be out in 2 weeks, are you anxious?" asked Samiksh.

"Well, not much really. I studied for months, the best I could, so we'll see however it turns out, it won't be bad," replied Vijay with a monotonous tone, which reflected his disinterest and lack of care about the results.

"yeah, of course, you have always been good at studies, at least better than me." said Samiksh with a slight smile.

"What does it matter though? Everybody talks about how important studying is and if you want to have fulfilling happy lives you must study dedicatedly and get better marks than every fellow student around you. But, what difference has my "good marks" made in my life?" said Vijay sarcastically, with a more colorful raised tone getting excited as he usually did before rambling his thoughts out loud.

"Not much I suppose? considering you are still here in the same village you were born in and talking to the same people you have seen a thousand times. And not to make assumptions about your life but I think it's more similar than different to what it has been for years." replied Samiksh with similar excitement in his voice.

"you are right! Nothing has changed, all these years of studying and getting the good grades we are supposed to and yet our lives are still like what they have been for as long as one can remember. For what's it worth, they have gotten duller and colorless at least when I was younger, getting a good score was something exciting and fun but now all the effort and toil doesn't even feel worth just a simple "A" letter. There's nothing new to the experience. One's mind can get numb to even the most joyful, satisfying adventures if done repeatedly like a silent mule, wasting away its life laboring for the same cause"

"and yet you spend months studying" interrupted Samiksh with a tired sigh.

"you speak the truth, that's the core of our problem! the misery one feels, is not caused by his inability to see the worth or satisfying element of achieving an empty reward, its caused by his inability to stop wasting away his days struggling for the same reward he finds so worthless; the reward being the good grade in our case. All our lives we have been conditioned to believe that, academic excellence, the good grades actually matter and will change one's life for the better, making it more satisfying when that's clearly not the case. But because that's what we have been told for years, and have spent so much of our lives getting good at fetching grades, we can't help ourselves from struggling, dedicatedly, numb to all other colors and aspects of life just to get a sliver of academic validation since that's the only thing we are trained at. Why does a man commended to death thinks, that if he had to live on a high rock on such a narrow ledge that he'd only have room to stand with the infinite ocean beneath him and everlasting solitude and darkness around him he would rather stand there for eternity than die. Why does the great greek warrior choose to fight in a battle that would earn him no riches, bring him no joy, and give him no relief but only curse him with loss, agony, pain, and death? When one is only educated in suffering, he's left with no choice but to seek institute in the suffering. Our misery is caused by our own inability to dream. However pathetic this may sound, but sometimes I feel envious of the students who attain the average grade and do not feel worthless and dejected for not being excellent in the textbooks they studied for a year of their lives. What a simple life it must be that's not wasted away, cramming impractical principles and texts, until the mind loses all its senses" rambled on Vijay in a confused frustrated voice, with words spilling out of his mouth so fast, as if his skull would have exploded if they stayed even a second longer inside his mind.

"That's a bit narcissistic of you," said Samiksh with a constrained smile "to be able to achieve excellent scores and be envious of your classmates who fail to even come closer. Why do you believe they don't have the same anxiety and stress as you about trying to excel academically after all they also have been trained to get excellent grades just like you, they just can't manage to. Imagine their disappointment with themselves!"

"I suppose you are right, to work so hard" Vijay was interrupted by a woman walking up the path in their direction, carrying a large bunch of grass on her head which covered her sweaty forehead. She was accompanied by a girl who appeared to be the same age as them. Their attention was mainly focused on her astounding beauty. She smiled softly through her soft pink lips, to greet them, revealing her pearl-white teeth. Her hair was dark as charcoal and her brown eyes glowed like embers. Her skin was spotless and soft as a winter morning. A true beauty! Enough to make any man forget his words, and the world around him, only to stand spellbound.

"Vijay and Samiksh! where are you two heading to?" asked the woman in an uplifting voice

"Oh nowhere special" muttered samiksh with glittering eyes and a wide smile "just walking down to the baori to fetch some water"

"That's good, the government pipelines are not any good, and gods! The water that flows out of them? It tastes of rust!" exclaimed the woman with disgust.

"Yes! Absolutely true! Nothing's better than some freshwater " replied Samiksh with an excited tone.

"Mother, we must head home. Father would be reaching home anytime now and lunch is yet to be prepared, he would be exhausted and hungry we mustn't make him wait for food" said the girl in a worried but soft voice.

"yes dear you are right, we really should head home now," said the woman and slowly started walking.

"we'll be on our way too now good-day to you," Samiksh said courteously and the boys continued their tread down the hill.

Vijay broke the silence with a haughty claim "oh how you have fallen for her!"

"what? fallen? for whom!" said Samiksh loudly with embarrassment

"Who? the girl of course, I recall all of us playing together when we were younger, I do not remember her name but she has grown to be enchantingly beautiful. Anyone would fall for her like you have" remarked Vijay feeling pleasure by the torment on his friend's face. He knew he was right and only planned to question him further for the sake of momentary joy.

"Her name is Siya and yes she is beautiful, but I, definitely am not in love with her" replied Samiksh haughtily trying to sound firm.

"You can't hide it from me, friend. Oh, how you smiled and turned red like an apple just by her presence, and the politeness in your voice! It all clearly shows on your face. You must like her very much and it makes sense too, as you must see her often and have made yourself believe you like her company as much you love her beauty"

"How harshly you pass your assumptions and judgments!" exclaimed Samiksh defensively with a serious look.

"Forgive me for I get too excited but tell me if I am wrong and you don't like the girl"

"No, your assumptions are all true, I do find her attractive as you said but I also like her company, she's smart, witty, and interesting. Contrary to what you might think, having a conversation with her is not boring and she has an intriguing worldview" Samiksh replied, his lips curved, even talking about her made him smile.

"I am sure she does."

"Don't be so sarcastic, you think I like her just because she's good-looking!"

"No, I think you do like her company and her abstract thoughts, but I believe her dark black hair and lovely eyes are what seduced your mind to develop an attraction to every part of her. The body and the mind, but I wonder if she looked.."

"you wonder if she looked less attractive, would I still enjoy her company" interrupted Samiksh getting more excitable but keeping his calm as he was aware, Vijay meant no offense and only liked talking about such matters to reach a deeper conclusion.

"would you?" asked Vijay getting more amused by the conversation.

"maybe. maybe not, but why is it a problem to like her for her beauty, after all, it's a part of who she is."

"It's not a problem, I'm sure half the guys in the village also love her for who she is and daydream about being with her. Just as you do. I just think it's a boring prospect" said Vijay while glancing at the yellow daffodils growing on the side of the mountain, he bent down and plucked one out from its stem. He continued walking, but his eyes intently focused upon the orange center of the flower as if looking for a hidden explanation of the cosmos, the stars, the beings, and existence itself.

"Boring?! Tell me, do you not enjoy the company of girls, do you not wish to be in love with a girl and spend your time with her?"

"of course I do, it's in my biological nature to seek attractive girls, talk to them and try to impress them. I just think highly beautiful girls or even things for a matter of fact are boring. It's the ugly, scarred, tainted sinners who experience life in all its true colors and hence are genuinely interesting"

"if beauty is so boring, then why are we all infatuated with it so much? Why do you look so intently at the beautiful daffodil in your hands"

"Aha, you are right we are obsessed with beauty," Vijay said with a smile on his face and took his gaze off the flower "Beauty seduces us on the path to truth. Beauty in itself has no moral nature but it can induce the greatest desires and emotions in men. Men have committed unforgivable monstrous sins for the sake of getting their hands on beauty. Why do the men of the greatest civilization, leave their castles and families to fight a bloody, savage ten-year-long war for the sake of a woman as beautiful as Aphrodite. All because of a prince being blinded by lust!! And what did Achilles fight for, he had nothing to win from the war"

"Nothing but Glory! a tale to be told all over the world and a legacy that would live for centuries" added Samiksh forgetting all about Vijay's initial judgments and getting intrigued by the discussion.

"Yes, a perfect tale! That's what it really is. We are consumed by the idea of perfection. The word has no definite meaning and yet so much has been lost for the sake of achieving perfection. Our minds are so obsessed with seeking perfection that we find it in anything, may that be women, stories, nature, architecture, and even death. What good does death bring to man and yet soldiers are awarded and glorified for dying brutally, all alone in pain, on cold battlefields. Why does the artist turn insane with mere brush strokes, just to capture a hint of beauty? We can't imagine anything being beautiful unless it's first perfect, and so our minds are seduced and tantalized to find perfection in the tiniest of petals and the greatest of mountains. But the word has no meaning, its nothing but an illusion and so the truth is lost in the pursuit of beauty" Vijay took a breathe and gave a look to Samiksh "and so the people who spend their lives in the pursuit of beauty while ignoring the truth that lies out there, are deemed madmen"

"or romantics!" replied Samiksh with a clever smile.

"Aah! so you consider yourself a romantic"

"Yes, it makes life a bit more... charming."

"So I suppose you'll continue trying to impress Siya"

"I think so, it keeps me busy and content. Should I not?"

"Oh no of course you should, what weight does any opinion has in front of a man's desires, maybe you'll fall in love, hopelessly. That would be tragic like all love stories are, and tragedies are the most compelling stories! So as long as her company makes your life interesting, I say pursue her with all your heart and effort!"

"or maybe she'll fall for me too" muttered Samiksh feeling stupid even thinking of something so hopeful.

"Such optimism! I might need the drugs you are on" Vijay said out loud and they both burst into laughter.

IV

Darkness

"It's absurd, right? To even think of something so serious when the woman obviously died of natural causes." Samiksh spoke in an irritated rough voice, his forehead turned into a mess of agitated lines.

"They spread rumors like wildfire just so they can keep themselves busy by involving in gossip and whispers. Even the thought of the woman being poisoned is so foolish... Careful! Don't slip into the tank" said Vijay to Samiksh who stood on side of the baori filling his two-liter bottles with clear fresh water and drinking some himself. The tank was not deep enough for anyone to drown in, but one still could hit his head on the steps inside it or could break his leg if they were to fall inside.

"And who do they believe is to be blamed for murdering the old woman? They must have their Villain! Someone who doesn't indulge in their nonsense discussions and the passive aggression which they call 'jokes'!" Vijay blurted out, letting out his loathe for the dull and infuriating attitude of the village folk towards each other, they all posed to respect and care for each other but he knew how they detested each other behind closed doors of their homes. He didn't despise their cold hate for each other but their refusal to express it on their faces and their continuous effort to hide it in their hearts and let it turn into an ugly, miserable, and hateful pile of feelings. How trapped they were in their sentiments, only if they could learn to let it go and be truly free.

"They believe it's the man that lives in the old brown house next to your grandmother's. He is to be blamed for her death"

"How did they even manage to reach such obscure reasoning?!"

"That I do not know" Samiksh screwed the caps back on his filled bottles and they both started walking away from the tank "I just heard my mother speak about it with some woman, before I could inquire about the details, she tasked me with fetching water"

"I see, well we must part ways now. I do not wish to walk up to the village as of now, so I shall spend some time treading a further bit down, where it's totally quiet" Vijay spoke softly while shaking Samiksh's hand.

"Of course, don't get lost somewhere. I'll see you later friend " Samiksh spoke warmly and walked away up the hill slope.

Vijay paced further down the rough dust covered road. He could see the path that led into the forest, covered with dark canopies of old fir trees spreading over miles and miles of land, untouched by any human. Bamboo plants seemed to grow out in bunch of five to ten at random points on the side of the forest with no apparent pattern to them. The thought of seeing a bamboo blossom struck his mind. He had never seen one in actuality but had intently researched about it on the internet one night. The flowers were nothing one would call beautiful, they were quite ordinary and in fact ugly in some ways. The petals were brown and dull and the flower appeared more like dried barley than a sublime bloom. Despite its drab colors and unattractive features, the flower was certainly special in a distinct way. Bamboos are known for blossoming only once in decades and the growth of their seemingly ordinary flowers was associated with death and destruction in ancient times. A mysterious ugliness that only revealed itself once in an eternity.

He slowly stopped and stood under a bamboo growing on the side of the path. He gazed at its long shoot, tilting his head up in the futile hopes of spotting one such flower. The slightest possibility of witnessing the erratic ugliness lurking beneath the green twigs and branches waiting to be noticed made him ruminate in the middle of a road; like a lost vagabond.

A car passed by, breaking him out of his delirium. After a second of thought, his feet seemed to move on their own, toward the woods. The trail that led into the forest was narrow, steep, and covered with patches of grass at spots where people never set foot. The trees colored the surroundings in dark shades of brown, with their old trunks cracking at every spot. He stepped cautiously avoiding the plethora of vicious stinging needles growing in the cover of bushes and shrubs. The sky had turned into hues of blue and black, making the thick forest appear even more mysterious, inviting, and sinister.

He kept walking towards the apparent nothingness. Into the blackness consumed by the inherent human urge to look into the abyss, stand on its edge, and sometimes even let go, to freefall into darkness.

He snapped out of his subconscious sea, on hearing a sound. A sound so subtle and muffled by the woods that one wouldn't even notice its presence in a normal state of mind.

He stood still and looked slowly around, even considering for a second that the sound was a mere facade of his mind. But then he heard it again! The same sound, it was no creation of his mind, the sound was real, a subtle nuance in a perfect stillness, arising somewhere deep in the woods. After intently focusing for a minute, he started walking away from the man-made path and onto the grass-covered strange trails of the forest.

He stepped one foot in front of the other, his heart getting anxious and mind weirdly excited by a strange spell. His breaths turned rapid as he could notice the sound getting louder and the distance between him and the source, decreasing with every step. In his haste to remove the cover of woods and reveal the true meaning of this strange mystery, he started running through the thorns and flowers all alike, lost in a frenzy.

After a few minutes of running around he eventually slowed down, his breath stopped and his heart sank as he had found the source, uncovered the mystery, and witnessed the horrible truth.

V

Death

He found himself standing in a small clearing between the thick woods and grass. The sound was as clear as day and it only took him a few steps more to discover a gut-wrenching scene. A brown cow lay flat on the ground in a pool of its own blood flowing out of a wretched wound near its hind leg, the flesh had turned dark and without the cover of skin, he could see its muscles torn and scrapped all over. The poor beast had found its way to the forest in search of long green grass and leaves to feed on but must have disastrously slipped on a rough rocky slope, broken its legs, and laid in the middle of nowhere helplessly, succumbing to pain and death. It could do nothing, except make that wretched wailing sound in the hope of being found and getting aided out of its misery. But it was all of course in vain, for no medicine and no doctor could save it, the body was already dead what remained was a sliver of its soul, holding on to its pointless life.

Vijay stood in horror and pressed his hand against his nose, as the pungent stench of death was all around. The cow noticed him standing next to its face, its eye twitched in agony and tears flowed down its hair-covered cheeks. With what was left of its strength, the dying beast breathed heavily, let out a blood-curdling low, and raised its head revealing the other half of its face; or what few shreds were left of it as its face had gotten infected with maggots and worms squirming around in its skull, feeding away on its eyeball, brains and rotting black flesh right down to the bones.

The sight was worse than Vijay's darkest nightmares, he could bear no more of it so he turned around and ran. With no sense or care of his direction, he ran for what felt like hours for all he wanted, was to escape from that horrendous site, where death loomed in the air but refused to put the poor being out of its misery and waited in a sadistic silence. He scrapped his leg against a bush of thorns but didn't pay it any notice as his mind was turned to that of a scared little child seeking safety from the dreadful reality of this terrible world.

He eventually found his way out of the blackness of that cursed forest and immediately threw himself on the ground. He sat on his knees with his face hidden in his hands. He panted for air, his chest felt blocked under an invisible infinite mass, and his face turned red. He shrieked in frustration, of being unable to help the agonized creature and running away like a coward, tears flowed down his cheeks. Time passed by and the reality carried on around him as he sat in the dirt, all alone with no care of this damned ill world.

VI

God

The sun was about to set somewhere on the horizon but it still wasn't dark yet. A soft wind blew through the valley and the crests, making a shrill sound as if nature itself was playing a gloomy tone on a broken flute. The temperature dropped notably as the night approached, people burnt the wood they had toiled for all day in mud stoves, to keep their fatigued bodies warm. In the evening the air smelled of smoke, making one's lungs heavy with every breath.

Vijay had returned back to the village and was walking aimlessly in an empty street with a slight limp in his left wounded leg and head hung low in dejection. He didn't wish to go home but to a silent, calm, and most importantly an empty place so he indecisively turned to the temple, for god's presence was something he didn't feel or cared for.

The temple was an old two-storied building colored in a light shade of pink with a bright red dome on its roof. The ground floor wasn't actually for worship, but a room for the temple priest who spent his time taking care of the property, keeping it clean, talking with the village folks who visited mainly on sacred days and festivals, and mostly praying. A flight of stairs led up to the first floor where a shiv linga resided, colored with red vermillion and always surrounded by a few coins which people left as an offering to God. Only young girls were allowed to take those coins as they were considered to be pure and a form of the goddess Durga.

Vijay stood near the stairs, staring blankly at the red dome of the temple feeling at rest and having no thoughts in his head. The place was quite yet filled with a presence he couldn't explain like a dead man's room. The wind blew softly making him shiver and sneeze, it was too cold to be out in the open at this time.

"It's getting cold outside, if you just want to be near the temple then might as well come to sit inside, near the fire, I was just about to make some tea. I'll make a cup for you too " said an old woman who seemed to appear out of the priest's room, with a serene smile on her face. Her hair was white as a dove and her old body with loose wrinkled skin was covered in an orange saree.

"Oh no, it's quite alright. You don't have to trouble yourself" Vijay replied hesitantly, startled by her sudden appearance as he didn't expect anyone to be there at this time and especially not an old woman.

"It's no trouble at all son, come just sit here by the fire and I'll get you some tea if anything you'll be saving me from my solitude for some time" the woman insisted, in such a kind gentle tone that Vijay couldn't refuse, so he walked towards the room, lit only by the fire burning in one corner inside a mud stove. He sat down next to the fire on an old rag while the woman sat opposite to him, as she added more milk and sugar to the boiling tea pan which sat on the bright orange flames.

"From the way you stood outside the temple lost in your thoughts, I take it you are not much of a worshipper." the woman said, again with the same gentle smile on her face.

"Oh, yes! I am not a believer in god myself" Vijay replied while looking around, inspecting the ill-lit room. A pile of old brown books, some of them missing their covers and pages, lay in the other corner on top of a bundle of clothes wrapped in a brown piece of rag. A blanket and dusty thin mattress, torn and chewed up by rodents were placed neatly in the center. The room itself was in no way cluttered or dirty, it was rather organized in an imperfect way. A few utensils such as plates and saucers were contained inside a cardboard box lying near the stove, along with a bundle of dried sticks and branches which the woman broke into smaller pieces with her weak thin hands and fed to the fire.

"How come you live here? Isn't this supposed to be a room for the temple priest?" Vijay finally let out the question, which had been bothering his mind since he saw the woman walk out of the room.

The woman chuckled softly "Yes you are right dear, it is a room meant for the temple priest's living but you see the priest who used to live here passed away a few months back, and I am his wife so I have been living here alone since then" her voice reflected a subdued sorrow as she mentioned about her late husband.

"if you don't mind me asking, how did he pass away?" Vijay questioned as his interest had been sparked by the situation he found himself in. He felt so intrigued to converse that he even forgot about expressing his half-hearted sorries about the priest's passing. And isn't the desire to know the story behind a tragic ending a better expression of one's genuine care than mumbling apologies and taking deep sighs?

The woman raised the pan off the fire and slowly poured the hot tea into two cups made out of clay. The stream of tea falling out of the pan, gleamed orange, reflecting the light of the hot embers. Steam rose out of the cups as they filled up nearly to the brink. She slowly offered one to Vijay and picked one up for herself. Her hands cupped the mud vessel to get warmth through its surface. They silently sipped.

"He suffered from T.B. and passed away the last December. Even in his last moments, he had lord's name on his tongue" she replied with a feeble smile, underneath which was concealed some disdain.

"I am sorry, T.B. sounds like he must have suffered even despite uttering the lord's name," he said sounding harsher than he would have wished to, for he couldn't help letting out his despise for God. He sipped the tea rather delighted with its flavor, it tasted of nostalgia. It reminded him of his father for a second. "The tea tastes really fine"

"He didn't pray to god to let him live. I believe he wished to be as close as possible to him, in his last moments on this earth before his soul rose to the heavens."

"Man can't even find peace in his own life, and hopes for it in death and the clouds!?" Vijay said with sarcasm and angst.

The woman let out a subtle laugh, seeing Vijay's frustrated young face. "Faith dear, faith is quite the power to make one live out his life away from depravity and suffering. My husband had never seen God or heard his voice, and he never claimed so. Yet he spent more than half of his life devoted to something greater than himself. He didn't think preaching God's name and reading scriptures will wash away his sins, but the simple act of having faith in a good spirit made him emulate that virtue in his own life, it kept him away from straying on the path of evil and he spent his days living a life of faith and hard work."

"That's quite convenient, to think God is just a righteous holy spirit"

"Why..? Do you believe God's evil? Doesn't that just makes life a bit more depressing for one?" her face turned worried and sad.

"Questions of God's nature or existence I think is not a matter of convenience or comfort. I don't believe God, even if he exists, is a truly virtuous spirit for anyone who holds the power of the cosmos in the palm of his hand could never be truly good. Power is a blinding force, it turns one sinful. No one ever gained power without bloodshed and sins. Being good in the moral and societal sense is only the capability of a weak man. Morals are the masks for weak men to hide their cowardice and God whether that be Krishna, Jesus, or Zeus loves to speak of his glory and mightiness so he's clearly not a weak being and definitely not a virtuous one!"

"Oh, you trouble your own mind with such thoughts. Why do you believe an evil entity commands us all?" the woman said in dismay and confusion.

Vijay lets out a subtle laugh "Oh that would be too terrible, yes, to think all the evil that already exists upon this earth is being controlled by a mighty supernatural evil being. That's why rather than believing in a devil disguised as a God living in the heavens, I choose to believe in no God at all...and even if I was to believe in God someday, I think more than good or evil he's indifferent. He pays no attention to our insignificant actions and we ourselves bring the suffering or blessings on us. A father who gave us consciousness and life only to abandon us in the hands of suffering, sickness, and death. Although now that I think about it, that would still make him a reckless selfish evil being. It's a rabbit hole, to think about his existence, so I prefer not to believe in him at all. But doesn't just the thought of God makes him all the more real, after all, he thrives on belief and thoughts!"

"You speak in such confusion! Oh, dear boy all these ideas and thoughts they'll never let your mind and heart be at peace, you think too much for your own good. Oh... I just pray and try to appreciate the good on this earth as long as am here!" the woman expressed in puzzlement as if Vijay's words had driven her own mind to dejected memories of the past.

Vijay sat in silence, sipping the hot tea. A cold breeze blew through the open window, making them shiver.

"oh, how forgetful of me to have left the window open." the woman remarked while trying to get up on her feet, to close the window.

"Don't worry" Vijay interrupted quickly while getting off the ground "I'll get it". He took a step towards the window but stopped in agony as his leg was wounded still and had not been tended to. With some slight struggle, he managed to shut the window and walked back to the fire.

"Wait! Oh, poor boy how you have hurt yourself, your foot! It's pricked by thorns, i didn't notice until now, my eyes are terrible in the dark" the woman said out loud in concern "But just stay there I'll pull them out and apply some turmeric on it for that will heal it faster and prevent any infection" she stood up on her frail legs and slowly walked towards the pile of books in the corner.

"There's no need to bother! it's just a few cuts and nothing more" Vijay cried hurriedly, feeling hesitant about revealing his leg and answering questions about how he got the cuts.

"yes it's just a few cuts so it won't be much trouble" the woman replied while looking through the bundle of clothes "I remember I kept it in here somewhere, for a situation just like this. Oh where is it..it must be here. Aha! Yes found it" she beamed excitedly on having found the turmeric contained inside a small plastic bag which was shut close with few black rubber bands.

Vijay stood awkwardly near the fire as the woman walked closer to him and sat down near his feet.

"Trust me it'll be alright you don't have to bear the trouble" He nervously dragged his foot backward but the woman grabbed it gently in her skinny cold fingers and placed it on her thigh.

"No need to feel shy, it'll just take a second okay? Just try to keep your balance while I remove these vile thorns. It might hurt a little but don't worry I'll be as gentle as possible " her hands and voice had a motherly concern and care in them. She slowly started plucking the blackthorns out of Vijay's sole. Blood had seeped through the skin and already dried up, creating scarlet streaks on his toes and heel. Vijay stood quietly, gazing at the small frail structure of the woman lit partially by the fire's light. He felt a strange warm sensation in his chest. The conflict and sadness in his heart seemed to disappear for a few moments with the woman's compassionate touch.

"I think I have removed all of them, but my eyesight is not the best so one can never be sure... In the morning check your leg once again in the sun for any thorns that I might have missed okay? Don't just let it be, it can cause you more pain later! All right now just give me a few seconds more, I'll apply this turmeric and then we'll be done with it" She removed the rubberbands and opened the packet's mouth. Cautiously she took out a pinch of turmeric from the packet and started gently applying it on Vijay's sole where the thorns were stuck.

"Yes, I'll definitely give it a look in the morning, and thank you very much for this" Vijay replied softly feeling relief from the pain. Suddenly he heard a sound coming from somewhere in the distance. A sound of people saying something in union and walking together. "Oh! I think they are finally taking the old woman's body for cremation"

"oh, are they...? Ah yes, I hear it too now! It sounds quite chaotic, there must be a lot of people. Alright, it's done, the pain should be all but gone by the morning " she said with a content look on her face while putting the rubberbands back on the packet's mouth.

"She was a lovely lady, Seeta. She always stopped by to have a conversation with me, after all she lived alone too. In fact, she visited the temple yesterday too! She appeared well and happy to me, it was rather shocking when I heard about her passing. Oh well, uncertainty is after all the vital aspect of life."

"They believe she was poisoned! How do they reach such absurd conclusions without any logic? Do you know who they accuse of the crime?" Vijay cried out, his mind back in its frustration.

"Yes.. they think it's Joseph, I believe he lives in the house next to your grandma's"

The revelation that the woman knew Vijay all along came to him as a surprise. Of course, she knew him! His grandmother used to bring him along to the temple when he was younger and too innocent to rebel against visiting the place, just for the sake of bowing in front of stones and pictures.

"Do you think there's some truth in this ?" Vijay asked trying to suppress his impulsive frustration and consider the situation rationally for a moment, however absurd it may seem.

"oh, I don't know... I am not one to trouble my mind with dreadful thoughts of things such as murders and that too of a woman dear to me. But.." her face turned morose and her eyes reflected dread.

"But..? but what! Is there something more to it?"

"Since I heard the talk about Seeta Devi being poisoned I haven't been able to drive this terrible thought out of my mind. Joseph too visited the temple at the same time as Seeta yesterday... He's a Christian yet he visits the temple, yes that might seem odd to some but I had seen him two, or three times standing outside the temple in the past too. He never really said anything or interacted with me or the priest whenever he visited. He just stood in silence at the temple stairs and never even went up, I think he just felt at peace here and liked to pray for a while. After all, the same God looks after us all from the heavens, so what difference does being at a temple or church make in one's prayers? I think he's also aware that other people won't look at it in the same way that's why he only ever came at dusk. They already hate him for no better reason than him being from a different religion and his face having scars and cuts on it...- I'll be honest his face does make me shiver whenever I see him. The thought of how he must have gotten all those horrible scars is a grim one. Anyways (she let out a deep sigh) yesterday when Seeta came, she asked me for a hot glass of water because it was too cold outside but by the time I walked outside with the water she had already gone upstairs to pray. And there he was. Joseph, standing outside, looking somewhere off in the distance, so lost in his own thoughts as if he wasn't even here. I requested him to give the glass to Seeta as my knees are weak and walking upstairs causes me pain that lasts for several days. He quietly went up and handed the glass to Seeta. Later she and I talked about some *shlokas* (lines) from the *Geeta* and she left for her house at dusk. Joseph too, although I didn't notice myself, had left sometime before Seeta did. I know this is very skeptical and paranoid of me but I can't shake the terrible feeling that... What if Joseph did manage to poison the water... Oh God, this is all so wretched! I feel sick even thinking about it!" her voice cracked and her face turned pale as she spoke about the horrifying idea.

Vijay stood near the door silently, thinking intently.

"I must go now, thankyou very much" He slipped his feet back into his black shoes lying outside the door and walked away into the street.

VII

Grief

After just a minute of walking, Vijay found himself on the street outside the sarpanch's (village head) house. The whole path was filled with a crowd of people, with men in the front and a group of women in the back. Seeta Devi's body which was wrapped in a white cloth and placed on a wooden stretcher was being carried on the shoulders of 2 men, one of them being her son who was accompanied by a priest wearing a saffron dhoti and cotton kurta. The priest held incense sticks in his hands and the men in unison chanted "Ram Naam Satya hai" (The lord's name is true). The daughter-in-law walked just behind the men, her hair loose and tangled in a mess, while she cried hysterically. The women around her comforted her in their embrace, but they too added to the chaos by letting out tears and sobs. Their faces were covered in sweat and tears, forehead frowned in dejection. Vijay scorned seeing the daughter-in-law's hysteria for it all seemed a pretend to him. "Why does she cries so loudly, what loss has she suffered? A woman she didn't ever come to meet in years!! It's a shameless act!" he thought to himself but didn't obsess over it too much as his mind was occupied with another idea, a more important one.

The Village sarpanch walked out of his home and bowed next to the body, while the son stood with his head hung low and eyes shut in sorrow. The sarpanch held the son's hand and uttered some words softly in his ears. The son replied only with a subtle nod.

He was reminded of the day of his father's funeral, he was fatigued after a long journey from Delhi in a congested Ambulance with his father's cold corpse. His grandmother had insisted on cremating him at his birthplace. His mother and he had arrived at the village early in the brisk cold morning. A group of men already waited for receiving them, and without much talking and discussion, he and another man carried the body in their numb hands to his grandmother's home. A group of women already waited for them with his grandmother who could be heard crying and wailing in pain from yards away. The rest of the day was spent in completing all the tedious rituals with a group of priests who made him utter prayers and mantras, which he did softly, in dejection and grief. A barber was called to shave his head with a cold sharp blade and finally, his father was cremated in the afternoon. Dark sick smoke rose high up, painting the sky in black sorrow. That day too the sarpanch had come. He stood close to Vijay and softly whispered in his ear with his hand on his shoulder "Now you must look after them, I am here if you ever need help"

"We should continue on our way now, for time is of the essence in matters such as cremation. It's about to be dark anytime now and it's a bad omen to cremate the dead after dark. Their souls fail to reach the heavens and are lost in the darkness!" The priest said out loud addressing the son and the crowd of men behind him. The priest's warning raised concern in everybody's mind and so the crowd resumed its slow, melancholic, walk of grief and chants of the lord's name.

Vijay stayed back, waiting for the gathering to pass and clear the street so he could continue on his journey. In a few minutes, the crowd was all but gone, except for a few men who had stopped behind at a turn and formed a sort of circle under the dark shade of a banyan tree. The men seemed to be discussing something in a heated manner but tried to keep their voices low, to avoid attracting unwanted attention. Vijay discreetly walked towards them in the darkness, as he couldn't help but find this gathering to be rather strange and suspicious. He stopped at a safe distance, hiding behind a wall while keeping his attention focused on the men in order to gain insight into their motives.

Despite his efforts, he could see nothing but aggressive hand gestures and hear incoherent mumbling. Just when he thought there was no use in standing behind the wall like a creep, one of the men said out loud in anger "He's a vile man! He has to pay for his wretched crimes!"

"Will you calm down?! Yes, you are right he's a vile man indeed. Have you seen the scars on his face? Nobody who sees his face would call him a gentleman!" said the other man trying to keep his voice low but in anger and excitement didn't realize it was too far from discreet.

Vijay listened intently as the discussion took a malevolent turn.

"They don't even mind cutting up a cow! He's nothing but a Godless man!"

"And we must not forget the unforgivable sin which he has committed yesterday! Poisoning an old woman?! Who does that except psychotic evil men? And Rakesh saw him at the temple with his own eyes, tell them Rakesh. Tell them everything you saw!"

"Yes... Yes. I saw it! I was just returning from the fields yesterday evening when I saw Joseph walking towards the temple and Seeta Devi was there too! Talking to the priest's wife. He definitely came there with evil motives!"

"Exactly! Otherwise, what business does a Christian has in a temple?! He never comes to any other functions in the village either. Just stays shut in his crumbling old house and roams around at dusk. I am telling you a man like that could never be up to any good."

"Okay, so it's decided, once the other people are back from the cremation we all must head to Joseph's house and make him answer for his crime! Till then we shall just wait at Rakesh's house."

All the other men agreed and walked away into another street, bringing the hateful conversation to an end. Vijay stepped out on the street from behind the wall, he had to hurry and reach at the old man's house before those men. Before all this turned into a violent, irrational, unjust display of hate. He had to get to the truth of the matter.

VIII

Monsters

The light was all but lost in the veil of darkness. The chaos and commotion of the day had faded with the sun, in the verdant hills somewhere. Only an eery quietness and calm was left behind. The narrow streets, only lit by the serene cold luminescence of a pale waning crescent moon were even harder to tread on. In the silence, Vijay walked slowly, with his ears wrapped in his scarf and hands inside his woolen pockets. The hollow sound of each step made him more sure of his objectives but simultaneously raised his apprehension. In the back of his mind, he had a sense of dread and a realization that his plans could bring dire consequences upon him. But like an artist prepared to lose himself in the efforts of expressing his erratic thoughts, he too was overcome with an irrational eagerness to make some sense of this bizarreness, confront Joseph, and possibly witness a darker reality.

After a difficult walk through the empty, dusty streets in an unsettling loneliness, he had finally reached the path that lead to his grandmother's house and to Joseph's too. He carefully walked down the slope that led to the fields, leaving behind his grandmother's bluish-dark home and heading closer to Joseph's infamous old house.

Being just a few steps away from the stairs that led down into the building's front yard, he could now see the small, crumbling home colored in old brown paint which was falling off in layers from the surface of its walls. He had seen the house many times in the past but only in his peripheral while heading off to some more important destination. In the dim light of the white incandescent bulb fixed outside the building on a rusty black pole, the house appeared less like a residence for humans to live and more like a skeleton of shadows crawling with broken dreams and horrible memories of the past.

Putting his afraid anxious thoughts, about this perilous idea of walking into a man's house who could possibly be a murderer and worse, at rest, he stepped down the four stairs and stood in front of the barren building.

The place was quiet as a graveyard with a strange sensation of sorrow in the air. Vijay tried to peek inside the house through a glass window that had turned blurry and blackish as a result of improper care. He could see nothing but just a glimmer of yellowish light from the inside. Instead of trying to knock at the door, he decided to first take a look around the house. The house was built in corner of a field, secluded from the rest of the village. On one side of the house, grew a pair of small trees, their leaves shuddered and rustled in the cold wind. Surprisingly along with the trees, also grew a yellow rose and bright pink bougainvillea plant. Both plants had a number of flowers blooming on them. Seeing flowers being grown and looked after in the backyard of a dark crumbling house, gave Vijay a slight kindling sense of hope.

"You are aware that it's disrespectful and invasive to get on another man's property without any permission?" said a deep voice from behind, startling Vijay.

He turned back to see a tall man in a black half-vest sweater with a white shirt underneath it. The cuffs buttoned up and the sleeves ironed neatly. His face looked mature rather than old; his skin had pores and wrinkles all over it as if he had been through years of physical effort, covered in sweat, mud, and grease, and left for the elements to wear him apart. And of course the scars. There were only three of them prominent enough; one ran down the side of his left cheek, and the second one was a burn mark on the right side of his forehead near the eyebrow, irregular and superficial like someone had hurled a burning piece of coal at him, the last and deepest of three was a long slanting cut from the bottom of his left ear to his throat, it had been stitched up rather improperly and had left behind a dark scar. The scars clearly gave him a distinct uncanny look but they were nowhere as terrifying as he had imagined them in his head; the worst monsters we confront are usually of our own creation.

"I am. I apologize to intrude in such a manner, but I have something of grave importance to discuss with you " Vijay tried to regain his composure so as to not look afraid or threatening but maintained a serious tone and distance.

"Intrude.. yes that you have and at an inappropriate hour. Before trying to indulge in any conversation with me I expect you would have the decency to introduce yourself, boy" he replied in a voice full of pride.

"Yes, of course, my name is Vijay. I live in the house next to you, and... It would be good if we discuss the matter at hand, so I can quickly get off your property" although he tried hard to appear stern his voice betrayed him, cracking with angst and the chill air.

"No. I don't think it's the time to have any discussion, Vijay. I would ask you to return to your home and leave me at peace too." his tone reflected a slight hint of threat. He turned his back towards Vijay and started walking to the door, having put the conversation at an end in his mind.

Vijay stood silent for a second, rethinking the whole situation and contemplating about returning back to his home and letting it be, for Joseph's calmness and poise glimmered of something completely opposite, something horrid and chaotic. But in the next second, he felt overtaken by the irrational frustration and eagerness to confront him and bring down the facade of composure and normality. He felt a baseless hatred towards him.

"They believe you murdered the old woman...Did you?" the moment he spoke he was overcome with regret for having said it at all. But now nothing could be done, he must go on. Joseph stopped in his place and slowly turned back. His face had lost its serenity, now he appeared aggravated.

"You must have no regard for ethics, to turn up at a stranger's house at night and hurl an accuse as vile as murder at him!" Joseph was clearly irritated but still tried to hold back his tone and kept his hands behind his back.

"I don't accuse you of murder but the rest of the villagers surely do. I have only come to question you about it and if you are innocent, warn you to save yourself from the group of vexed men with no good intentions who could be here anytime" Vijay felt a weird excitement as he thought that Joseph was now at least ready to speak with him.

"Oh, the shallow senseless villagers! They find no contentment in their tedious lives so, of course, they paint me as the scoundrel in their whispers. The men are fed up with working in the fields and irritated by the whining of their wives and children. The wives are tired of their unfulfilled wishes for a fancy lifestyle, so they despise their husbands and are jealous of each other. They have nothing better to do than toil away their lives in the dirt and chitchat! I don't expect their minds to be occupied by anything but foolish ideas and senseless anecdotes" Joseph said in a raised tone with his face partially lit by the moonlight giving him a ghostly pale look.

"That's true, they do talk nonsense but they must have reasons to loathe you to such a level that they think you to be capable of even murder!" Vijay raised his tone too but tried to keep his calm to avoid offending the man. But in finding the truth in matters so serious, the offense was unavoidable and often necessary.

"I don't care what they or for a matter of fact you think!" his face turned grim and his still calm posture was gone. Now he was visibly angered and didn't care to hide it.

"I am sure you don't," Vijay said softly feeling frightened and hesitant by the sudden change in the man's demeanor. "but you don't speak with anyone else in the village or ever attend any of the events, I think that makes you more susceptible to being treated as the strange, uncanny outsider"

"I have no interest in their events and why would I care to speak with any of them? They never cared for me or my family so why should I bother about them? I live my life in peace and I have nothing to prove to anyone! It would be better if you stop questioning me and get out of my land" he raised his left hand in the air pointing towards the stairs and madly staring down at Vijay.

Vijay stepped back feeling terrified of his coarse voice and raised temper. But like great disparity seems to spark greater hopes, Joseph's hatred and anger brought up Vijay's own bitterness and frustration to the surface.

"Peace?! You in no way look to me at peace, instead, you look full of anguish and despise. If you don't care for what the villagers think, then why do you detest them so much?" They loathe you and you reflect that back." he said out loud, his voice filling the peaceful night with its hollow vexation. The words coming out his mouth attacked his own conscious as if in the attempt of lighting Joseph's darkness he had set his own afire; to which he had been ignorant for days and now it slowly but surely burnt towards an impending outburst.

"What do you know about me? Nothing. Yes! I am not at peace and how can I be, in a place where people dislike me for whatever reasons they can find whether that be my scarred ugly face, my religion, my denial to indulge in their fancy facades, my loneliness, and when they are bored of all that, they cook up a story and blame me for the death of an old woman?! I am not concerned with any ideas, you or the rest of them want to create in your heads, but I didn't kill that old woman. I have never even met her in my damn life!" his throat turned hoarse and dry with every word he uttered in anger. His voice was so harsh it made Vijay's ears hurt as if nails had been pricked in them.

"But you saw her yesterday! At the temple and you even handed her a glass of water, which people think you poisoned, and that's how you killed her." Vijay confronted him with the fact, which took him by surprise as if he had forgotten about everything that happened before this conversation.

"Oh, you fools! Yes, I met her at the temple but I barely spoke to her. Why would I kill a woman for no reason at all? Why do those bastards reach such wretched conclusions about me?"

"Because you are a hateful man, who continues to spark hatred for himself in every man's heart just because he can't live with himself!" Vijay uttered those words in a loud monotonous shout. His soul turned cold as he was hit with a terrible realization.

IX

Depravity

The night again turned silent but only for a second. Joseph and Vijay stood under the stars and cold darkness, staring at each other in hate, anger, loathe, and bitterness. Their bodies were perfectly still but the skin twitched with the hot blood rushing underneath it. Their faces were so pale they appeared green and their hands clenched into fists. The veil of quiet and solemn attitude was gone and the inherent animal frenzy had started to reveal itself. In that dim moonlight and the darkness which surrounded them, they appeared nothing less than insane men. The whole scene had a sort of divine madness to it.

"Hate? You don't know the first thing about hate" said Joseph with a subtle chilling laugh and then he started shouting "Yes I hate them all! Every single one of them! They think so highly of themselves and look down upon every man they see... And their pride! They think their lives are hard and terrible so they are above everyone else, so blinded! They don't have the slightest idea about how truly terrible life is... When you have to see a man you spent years of your life with getting burnt, his skin melting away from his face, by some wretched trap he happened to step into, that's what's truly terrifying! (his voice cracked in pain)When he lies in your arms staring at your face with eyes so dark and a gaze so intense, it feels like it's murdering your soul!! He tried to utter words out of his mouth but in vain because half of it had already melted away, tears flowed down on his burning skin, and his eyes begged for death!" He paused for a second taking a breath with terrible difficulty "and oh my son! My dear boy Matthew! He died in front of my eyes and all I could do was scream and watch... Yes I remember it clearly, I stood right here banging at this window (he walked towards the window and tapped it hard with his knuckles, making a shrill sound) I cried and begged him to open the door but he stood inside with no expressions whatsoever on his face like he wasn't even here. I banged my fists on the door and the windows trying to break them open, as he hung himself from the fan with one of his mother's saree, right inside that room in front of my eyes. It felt like.. with my every scream and attempt to get in there and stop him, he only got more eager to tie that noose around his neck with hands still as a gunman; as if he was escaping from me. Yes! He was petrified of me, my face and just my presence made him so quiet out of fear. Oh, my own son hated me! None of these villagers even showed up the day he died, none of them ever even noticed or cared to ask. I buried him in the fields all alone in the evening and none of them cared! And my wife, oh Jessica! She was always quiet around me out of respect and fear but after Matthew's death, she stopped talking to me at all out of hatred. She always used to carry around a piece of that wretched saree and fell into a quiet depression. Oh her heart and soul died the day her son did the sickness merely killed her body. But, I! I am still here! Me! The one who truly deserved to burn, rot and die was left behind! The people, the war, the death it's all just a twisted play, the vilest and most hideous with no shred of justness!"

Joseph finally stopped, breathing heavily, his face turned scarlet with the scars appearing more deep and vicious than they did before. Even despite the numbing cold, sweat poured down the top of his forehead as he stood with his hands shuddering with angst and exhaustion; drops of dark blood dripped down on the dirt, flowing out of his knuckles which he had managed to cut while furiously tapping on the glass window.

Vijay stood in shock and horror, all his frustration and anger had now melted into the grief and misery which he had hidden, in some deep crevice of his mind for months. He was overcome with raw emotions, burning his insides, his very soul; he could no longer hold them within, for the guilt and agony were enough to consume him. His legs trembled and he felt sick to his core, with a sudden jerk he fell back on the flight of stairs and hid his face in his palms as if what he was going to express was too horrible to be revealed to the naked eye. He let out a blood-curdling cry, so loud and painful as if it came not from his throat but from his crippled conscience.

"I killed him! I murdered my own father! I consented to his death like a cruel cold bastard!! I have committed the vilest of sins. There's no hell, no punishment torturous enough for a monster like me!" tears flowed down his eyes and wretched wailing ripped through his chest "He loved me more than his own life and showered me with all the comforts he could afford to and I, his devilish son took his life in an instant. Oh the suffering that fell upon us! How he went into the hospital thinking it would all be normal in a matter of days and how it swiftly turned into the worst nightmare of our lives. Oh, my poor mother! She served him every second, smiled in front of his dying eyes but at night cried in such grief and sorrow, it burnt my very soul. The doctors! They pierced him with needles and with the blood, every day sucked a shred of his existence. Oh, my father, the dying sick man even in such pain comforted me... hoped for it to all be better, promised me that he'll defeat the vile sickness and overcome it! Mother prayed for months, pleaded, and begged God for his life. They both faced suffering no matter how much anguish and misery it caused them! And I a tiny, shallow, godless boy succumbed to it the first chance I got! Those idiots why they had to put that decision on my terrified weak conscience? He was in such pain and they said there was no hope for him, that I must consent, for his treatment was causing no good but only making him suffer more and it would cost my poor mother a fortune, we couldn't bear to pay! They said he had no chance and I gave up on him just like that! I couldn't even afford hope for my own father! With my one word, I stole the slightest chance he had at life. I signed those papers and they left my father devoid of any hope or God, alone in the hands of death! I am no man, but a malevolent monster!!"

"God!? He's a devil with a false name. If he was truly virtuous he would have never let such suffering fall upon us, he would have never created vicious beasts like us! He would have erased our existence from the face of this universe the day man turned treacherous and committed the first sin! Instead, he left us to.." Joseph revealed a silver chain from beneath his shirt, a copper cross hung at the center of it "rot, suffer and die" Drops of tear flowed down his scarred cheeks, his eyes forcibly shut in frustration. He pulled at the chain furiously, and drops of spit came out of his mouth as he spoke madly in anger, his face twisted and turned in sheer hate and despise as if all the evil in the world had possessed him in that moment "He is no God of mine!!" The chain broke with a snap and he hurled it violently to the ground.

Vijay stared at the cross lying in the dirt. His face was wet and wrinkled with tears and grief. To his immense shock, he felt a sense of calmness within him. A quite, placid releif. His soul didn't ache and his heart didn't feel feverishly burning for the first time in months.

Both of them remained silent for a split second, lost in their minds but then they heard the sound of footsteps and a group of men loudly talking, approaching them. They both knew who the men were and what grave danger they were in.

Joseph acted swiftly and shouted, "Boy, get the hell out of here!" He walked inside the house. Vijay quickly got back up at his feet, he was about to run but stepped back and bent down to pick up the cross. Joseph reappeared, holding a dark object firmly in his left hand; Vijay realized in an instant, it was a gun.

"Run now! Go away you fool!" Joseph yelled at the top of his voice with concern on his face.

Vijay climbed up the stairs as the men finally emerged from the darkness, standing on top of the slope with metal rods in their hands. He didn't wait for a second more and ran towards the fields as fast as his legs allowed him to. A gunshot echoed through the hills. He glanced at the cross reflecting the moonlight, clenched it within his fist, and closed his eyes. He ran with no sense of direction into the dark barren dirt with the cross still in his hands and faith in his heart that he will be safe.

FAITH

May 10th 2016

I still get terrifying nightmares of that day sometimes, but other than that I feel at rest. The anguish and pain are all gone, what's left is grief, his beautiful memories, and the unexpressed love in our hearts. Mother has started to smile again. It might not be often but I catch her sometimes looking at her and father's pictures, and smiling softly with tears in her eyes. The emptiness he has left behind may never be filled and serve as a constant reminder of the true master that death is. But despite being the servant of death, I must not forget, that only after one dies can he truly be reborn, that the essence of life is not in its mortal nature but it lies in the immortality of our spirits. I find a warm sensation within me, it's not hope but faith I think. I have faith that death is not a path to nothingness, but a deliverance of freedom and an opportunity to shed our illusions of the ego and be reborn as what we truly are; a fragment of the infinite universe. I struggle with these thoughts often and find myself filled with angst and anger, for the spark of this faith is still weak and may remain like that for years to come. But at least I now have it somewhere within my soul, kindling and thriving in there, leading me on the path of forgiveness and keeping me from running astray into hate and depravity.

"Faithless is he that says farewell when the road darkens"

- J.R.R TOLKEIN

Author's Note

I'll try and be brief with this. It's easier to make characters speak your thoughts but terribly difficult to do it yourself, it's too personal, too exposing. I suppose that's why I feel more hesitant while writing this than I did before while writing all that bizarre stuff. This story while being fiction is based much on reality, personal experiences, and confused ideas; I think that's good, after all, a story without truth at its core is just a mere facade of senseless words. Ideas about God, Death, and Evil have always fascinated me but without an experience of witnessing Death, I now realize how naive those ideas were. After some tragic weeks, I think I have a, certainly not deeper but at least better understanding of Death and suffering. I am not a very optimistic or religious person as I am sure you could understand from the little story, but I have started looking at life with more faith. I often wondered what's the difference between hope and faith. Aren't they just two names for the same tiny irrational optimistic feeling in our hearts? But I have started to understand that the difference might be subtle but it does exist. I think Jim carry explained it the best "Take a chance on faith. Not religion but faith. Not hope but faith. I don't believe in Hope. Hope is a beggar. Hope walks through the fire and Faith leaps over it" Both hope and faith are based on believing in some greater force. The only difference between the two is; Hope is believing what you want will magically happen for you, meanwhile, faith is first taking a step forward, making an effort, and then believing that what you want will happen. And what about God? Well, personally I still don't believe in that old man and I don't ever pray. But in my moments of dejection and meaninglessness, I find myself with a desire to quiet down, stop thinking, sit on my knees and call to some greater force than this mortal existence. Ironically, isn't the desire to pray a prayer itself? I think I should stop now or my struggling conscience will ramble on for a few more pages. Finally, I am grateful to you, for buying this little novella and reading it till the end. My words will have fulfilled their objective if you found some meaning and truth in them. Thank you from the bottom of my troubled heart.

Cordially

Arun

9 798889 090397

Printed by Libri Plureos GmbH in Hamburg, Germany